Play with Clay!

It was

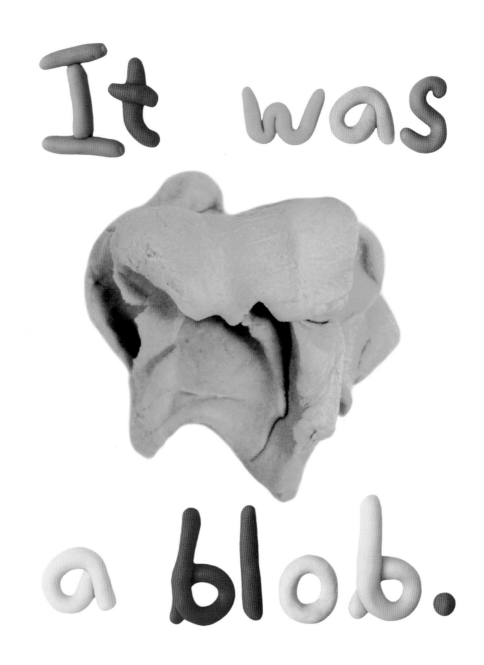

a blob.

Until I

formed

it...

Until I

rolled

it...

It was a snake.

Until I coiled it...

It was a flowerpot.

Until I broke it...

It was

lots of
little pieces.

Until I

Made

them into
something new...

It was a flower.

Until I

it...

It was

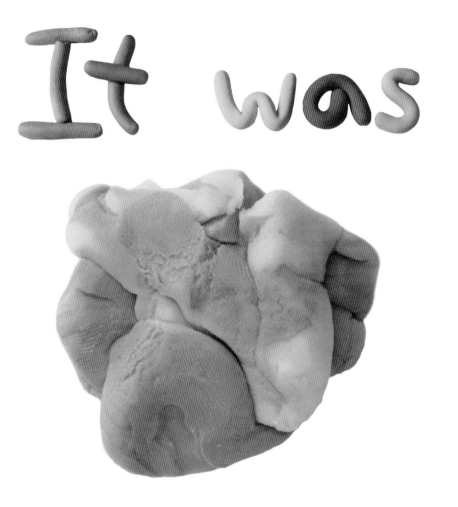

pink and yellow.

Until I

mixed it...

It was

an orange.

Until it wasn't...

It was

so many
things.

Until
time

next